The Three
Princesses

The Three
Princesses

and other classic fairy-tales

Retold by Fiona Waters

Illustrated by
Gail Newey

BLOOMSBURY
CHILDREN'S
BOOKS

For Sarah, with much love

First published in Great Britain in 2000
Bloomsbury Publishing Plc, 38 Soho Square, London, W1V 5DF

The moral right of the author has been asserted
A CIP catalogue record of this book is available from the
British Library

ISBN 0 7475 4714 9

Printed in England by Clays Ltd, St Ives plc

10 9 8 7 6 5 4 3 2 1

Contents

The Witch and the Sun's Sister

A story from Russia

Long ago in the time of the wolves there was a Tsarevich called Ivan who was a fearless horseman. One day when he was in the stables rubbing down his magnificent horse after a wild ride over the steppe his groom, Mikula, said,

'I have had a very strange dream,
Tsarevich. I dreamed you had a new
sister who was in reality a witch.
She had fearsome teeth and wicked
ways, and she devoured you, your
father the Tsar and your mother the
Tsarina and everyone in your
household.'

Ivan just laughed and told Mikula he must have taken too much vodka to dream such wild things and he went into the palace for his evening meal.

Imagine his surprise when his old nurse came bustling up to him with the astonishing news that the

Tsarina had just been delivered of a baby girl. He went in to look at his new baby sister and with a thrill of fear he saw she had been born with a full set of very sharp teeth, and as she looked on him there was a wicked gleam in her green eyes.

Ivan wasted no time. Running out of the palace, he quickly saddled up his horse and galloped off into the night. He had no idea where he was going but he knew he had to prevent the prediction of Mikula's dream from coming true. He galloped like the wind and as dawn was breaking he spied a tumbledown cottage with a thin

wisp of smoke rising from the
chimney. He opened the door, and
peering inside, he saw two ancient
women sewing as if their lives
depended on it. He told them his
strange story and asked if they
could help him.

'Alas, dear Tsarevich, we cannot help you. When we have worn out all our needles and sewn all the thread on this reel we will die.'

Ivan wished the old seamstresses well and continued on his way, galloping faster than ever. As he

looked into the distance he saw a
huge man pulling up trees by their
roots. He stopped to tell his strange
story and asked the man if he could
help him.

'Alas, dear Tsarevich, I cannot help you. As soon as I have pulled up the last of these mighty trees I will die.'

Ivan wished the huge man well and continued on his way, galloping even faster than before. As he looked into the distance he saw a great giant turning the mountains over. He stopped to tell his strange story and asked the giant if he could help him.

'Alas, dear Tsarevich, I cannot help you. As soon as I have re-arranged this mountain range I will die.'

Ivan wished the giant well and

continued on his way, galloping,
galloping. Dusk was falling and as
he galloped into the sunset, the
Sun's sister bent down, swept him
into her arms and carried him off up
into the sky. She offered him food
and drink and after he had tended

to his poor weary horse, the
Tsarevich told the Sun's sister his
tale.

Now the Tsarevich was a
handsome young man and, as we
have seen, a kindly man so the Sun's
sister resolved to keep him by her

side for she was lonely. She treated him like her very own son and he wanted for nothing, but he could not forget the peril his family were in. He looked down at his father's palace and saw that all lay in ruins. His sister the witch had devoured everyone and laid waste to all the lands about the palace.

When the Sun's sister found him, his eyes were full of tears.

'Why are you crying?' she asked.

'It is only the wind in my eyes,' Ivan replied.

'I will stop the wind,' said the Sun's sister and she commanded the wind to cease blowing.

Three times she found him with tears in his eyes and three times she quelled the wind, but then she realised that it was not the wind filling his eyes with tears but his deep unhappiness. The Tsarevich told the whole story of his sister the

witch and the Sun's sister decided
to help him. She gave him three
parcels with instructions to open
them only for friends. Thanking her
for all her kindness, the Tsarevich
took his leave from the Sun's sister
who gently placed him back down

on the earth where she had found
him.

He retraced his footsteps and the
first person he met was the giant,

who by now had only one more
mountain to overturn.

'Perhaps I can help you,' said the
Tsarevich and he gave the giant one
of the parcels. When the giant
opened it he found a small rock
which he dropped on to the ground.
Straightway there was an endless
range of mountains stretching as far
as the eye could see. The giant was
overjoyed and promised the
Tsarevich he would always be ready
to serve him.

Ivan set off once again, and
before long he met the huge man
who now had only one more tree to
uproot.

'Perhaps I can help you,' said the Tsarevich and he gave the huge man the second parcel. When the man opened it he found a comb which he dropped on to the ground. Straightway there was a vast forest stretching as far as the eye could see. The huge man was overjoyed and promised the Tsarevich he would always be ready to serve him.

Ivan set off once again and he soon reached the cottage where the two old seamstresses were down to their last needle and only a hand's span of thread.

'Perhaps I can help you,' said the Tsarevich and he gave the two old

ladies the last parcel. When the parcel was opened out fell two small apples. The old ladies each took a bite and straightway there were reels and reels of thread and thousands of needles. The old ladies

were overjoyed and promised the Tsarevich they would always be ready to serve him.

Once again Ivan turned his steps back the way he had come until he reached the palace which was now

just an empty shell. As he walked through the ruined corridors his sister suddenly appeared before him.

'Dearest brother, you have returned at last! I must prepare a feast for you,' and there was a wicked gleam in her green eyes as she turned to leave the room.

No sooner had she swept out of the door than a tiny mouse scuttled out of a hole in the wainscoting and squeaked,

'Fly, fly, Tsarevich! Your evil sister has gone to sharpen her teeth!'

Ivan thanked the mouse and dived out of a broken window, fleeing down the path as if all the devils in

hell were after him. Soon he heard
his sister, hot on his heels, and he
ran even faster. He reached the
seamstresses' cottage and begged
them to help him. As he ran by, the
old ladies dropped their sewing

30

behind his heels and a huge lake
spread out as far as the eye could
see. Ivan was far ahead by the time
the witch had swum across, but
soon she was pressing close again.

He reached the huge man

uprooting the trees and begged him to help. As Ivan ran by, the huge man threw up a vast pile of trees which completely blocked the road. By the time the witch had tossed all the trees aside, Ivan was well ahead, but soon she was pressing close again. With a great effort, Ivan put on a spurt and reached the giant overturning the mountains and begged for his help. The giant piled three mountains all on top of each other and by the time the witch had climbed all the way up one side and all the way down the other, Ivan was well ahead. But soon the witch was pressing close again.

Now the Sun's sister had been
watching the Tsarevich's efforts and
she could see he was tiring fast. She
bent down and scooped up the
witch and threw her high over her
shoulder up into the sky, and the
wicked sister was never seen again.

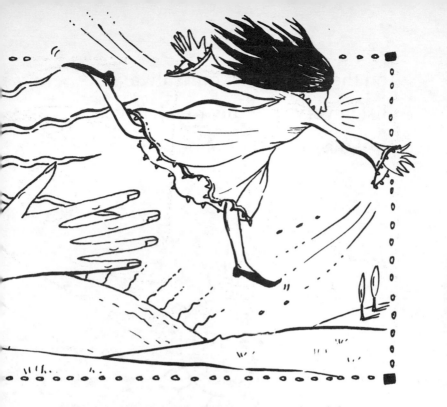

Then the Sun's sister breathed her
warmth down on to the ruined
palace and in an instant all was
restored again with the Tsar and the
Tsarina on their thrones and the
Tsarevich in the stables grooming
his trusty horse. And from that day

on the Tsarevich would always
listen very carefully to whatever
Mikula had to say about his dreams!

The Three Princesses

A story from Spain

Many years ago when Spain was
ruled by the Moorish princes, there
lived a King who so loved his three
beautiful daughters that he could
not bear the thought of ever losing
them. He built a narrow steep tower
high up on a glass mountain and, as

if that were not deterrent enough, he
placed three enchanted horses by
the foot of the tower. These great
beasts had huge flashing hooves

that would surely trample to death anyone foolish enough to attempt the climb up to the three sisters.

Many brave knights came to try their luck in capturing the sisters but all were either defeated by the glass of the mountain or the huge height of the tower. Some perished under the driving hooves of the enchanted horses. The King grew so confident that he promised his daughters in marriage should anyone manage to rescue them. Now one day three brothers from the North arrived in the region, determined to succeed where all others had failed.

The youngest brother, called Don Carlos, rode some way behind the other two and when they galloped off to the foot of the tower, he found his way to the market where he made some very peculiar purchases. First he bought a huge cart with two sturdy oxen, then a thick rope a mile long, and thirdly a big bag of long nails and a hammer. People laughed at him, but as you will see he knew a thing or two.

It was not long before he met his two brothers, looking very crestfallen. They had been quite unable to scale the mountain or the steep sides of the tower and had

only just escaped the great
enchanted horses. When they saw
Don Carlos riding in the cart drawn
by oxen they mocked him:

'Foolish brother! Whatever makes
you think you could succeed where
we have failed, and why are you

driving that preposterous cart?'

'You can laugh at me if you will,'
replied Don Carlos, 'but I am the
one who will succeed in this quest.
Come with me and you shall have
two of the princesses for your
brides.' This bold promise only

43

made the brothers laugh even more, but as you will see Don Carlos was to have the last laugh.

When they had all reached the foot of the mountain, the two elder brothers flung themselves down on the grass and waited to see what Don Carlos would do. First he tied the thick rope around his waist with a clever knot, and then he hung the bag with the long nails round his neck. Then he took the hammer and drove one nail deep into the glass side of the mountain. He placed one foot on this nail and drove in another, higher up, and then placed his other foot on this one. And so he hammered and climbed, and hammered and climbed, and eventually he reached the door of the narrow tower. He knocked loudly on the door and suddenly there in front of him stood the most beautiful girl he had ever seen. It was the youngest princess.

'How ever did you manage to climb this dreadful mountain? My sisters and I were put here by our father who does not wish anyone

ever to take us away from him.'

Her sisters came to the door at the sound of voices and Don Carlos could see that they were also very beautiful. He was delighted that he and his brothers should have such lovely brides.

'I am here to save you. You must do as I tell you and you will soon reach the ground unharmed.'

But the sisters were afraid of the enchanted horses.

'You must go back while there is still time. There are three terrible enchanted horses guarding us and they will trample you to death,' said the youngest sister.

But Don Carlos knew a thing or two and without any more ado he quickly tied his rope round the waist of the eldest princess and lowered her gently over the side of the mountain. Down, down she swung until she reached the foot of

the mountain, to the great
astonishment, and delight, of Don
Carlos' two brothers. The second
sister was lowered in just the same
way, but just before it was the turn
of the youngest sister she turned to

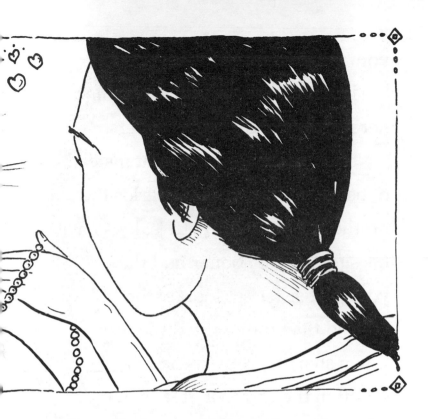

Don Carlos and slipped a string of
pure river pearls round his neck,
saying,

'This is but poor thanks for
rescuing us but you should never
part with it as one day it will save

you,' and she too made her way to the bottom of the mountain to join her sisters and the two brothers.

Now I am sorry to say that instead of being grateful to Don Carlos the brothers were filled with jealousy at his success. No sooner had the youngest sister set foot on the ground than they pulled the rope down sharply from his hands and set off in the cart in a great cloud of dust, taking all three girls with them. They galloped like the wind to the court of the King who was greatly astonished (and very angry) to see his daughters. He ranted and shouted and banged around but it

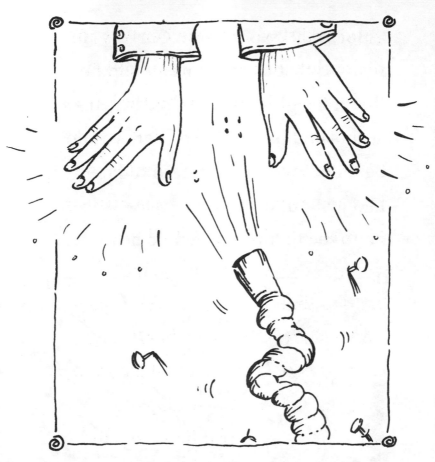

was no good, he had to keep his
promise. And so it happened that
the eldest daughters were married
to the eldest brothers.

But what of poor Don Carlos? He realised that by the time he climbed down the glass mountain again the sisters and his fickle brothers would be miles away, but undaunted he had just put one foot over the side on to the first nail when he heard a

great snorting and trampling.
Whirling round, he was confronted
by the three enchanted horses
galloping furiously towards him. He
closed his eyes and gave himself up
for lost, but just as he felt their hot
breath on his face they all came to

an abrupt halt right in front of him. He opened one eye cautiously as a large nose nudged his shoulder and he heard a gentle whicker of pleasure. The largest of the three horses was right by his side but clearly had no intention of harming him.

'How can this be?' wondered Don Carlos. 'Why have they not trampled me to death?'

To his utter astonishment the horse bent his great head and whispered in Don Carlos' ear,

'You are wearing the magical river pearls of the youngest sister. We are here to help you escape. Jump up on

to my back and hold on to
my mane very tightly.'

Well, Don Carlos was astonished,
but he scrambled up on to the great
shiny back of the horse and buried
his hands deep in his mane. With

a great whinny of triumph the
horse sprang over the side of the
mountain. For the second time in as
many minutes Don Carlos gave
himself up for lost but the huge
horse glided down the side of the
mountain as lightly as a feather and

landed on the ground. As Don Carlos slid off, the horse bent his head down again and whispered,

'Pluck a hair from my mane, oh Master. If ever you need help blow this hair up into the air and I shall be by your side,' and so saying the

horse rose up in the air again and was gone before Don Carlos could draw breath. He put the horse hair away carefully in his pocket and set off to walk to the court of the King. He arrived long after the wedding feast was over, and the only glimpse he had of the sisters and his brothers was when they rode through the town in a great procession. But he noted with great pleasure that the youngest sister did not appear to have found a husband yet.

'I shall wait and see what is to be seen,' said Don Carlos to himself, and he went to work as a shepherd in the King's great meadows. Now

after about a year news came that the King was losing his sight and none of his court magicians or doctors could cure him, so he had sent out a proclamation that

whoever could restore his sight should have the hand of the youngest princess in marriage. Don Carlos carefully took out the horse hair from his pocket and blew it up into the wind and instantly his magnificent friend was pawing the ground in front of him.

'Master, how may I help you?' asked the horse.

Don Carlos explained that here was an opportunity for him to gain the hand of the youngest sister if only he could find a cure for the King's blindness.

'This is simple, my Master. Far away in India there is a fountain which flows with magic water. I will fetch some of this water for you and you will achieve your heart's desire,' whispered the horse.

Don Carlos could scarcely believe it when in the twinkling of an eye the horse stood once more in front of him with a flagon of the precious water in his mouth.

'Some day I will try to repay you, dearest friend,' but the horse only snuffled in his ear and bid him hurry to the King's court.

Now when he arrived the guards were very reluctant to let him in for he looked so poor and shabby, but the King heard all the commotion in

the courtyard and when he was told
that there was a young man
claiming to have a cure for his
blindness, he ordered the guards to

let Don Carlos in immediately. For
truth to tell he was very weary of his
dark hours. You will remember he
was not a very patient King.

'Come, young man,' he snapped.
'Though I have no reason to
believe you will have any more
success than all the other charlatans

who have tried before you.'

So Don Carlos poured some of the water on to a clean white cloth and wiped the King's eyes. The King sat completely silent for a moment and then leapt to his feet with a great shout,

'I can see again! I can see!'

As you can imagine, the rejoicing was enormous and, hearing all the noise, the princesses came running into the room. The youngest spied the string of river pearls round Don Carlos' neck and knew immediately this was the brave man who had rescued her from the glass mountain. When the King heard the whole story he was so angry with the two brothers that he banished them (and their wives) from his kingdom for ever. Don Carlos and the youngest sister were married and the King made Don Carlos Prince Regent. And what of the enchanted horses? Well, Don Carlos

had not used all of the water from
the magic fountain on the King's
eyes so he poured some over each of
the horses and straightway they
were transformed into three brave
knights and they all lived in great
contentment together for many
years.

The Children of Lir

A story from Ireland

When magic still worked there lived
in Ireland a King and Queen of the
Tuatha Dé Danann who had four
children and they all lived happily
together. But one dark day the Queen
died. The King, Lir, was heartbroken
and despaired for his family.

'Don't worry, Father,' said
Finnuala, the daughter. 'I will look
after my brothers.'

But Lir knew that children needed
a mother so he resolved to marry
again. His wife's sister, Aoife,
arrived one summer day and took
the whole family down to the lough
side for a picnic. She made the
children laugh and looked at Lir
with her dark deep eyes and they all
fell under her spell. Ere long the
King married Aoife and for a while
all was well. Aoife laid up chests of
new clothes and Lir went fishing
with his sons and swimming with
Finnuala. But Aoife soon tired of all

her new finery, she wanted Lir to
spend more time with her and as
time went by she became more and
more jealous of the children.

'Lir loves those wretched children more than me. I must do something to rid us of their constant presence,' she murmured to herself as she gazed at her beautiful reflection in the mirror.

She suggested to Lir that the

children might be sent away now
that they were growing up, but Lir
would have none of it.

'They are as much a part of me as
my right hand. I could not bear to be
without them,' he said and left Aoife
seething as he went off to take the

children riding. Time and time again she tried to persuade Lir to travel with her, leaving the children behind. But Lir would have none of it. And so her bitterness grew to be a great wickedness in her heart and she decided to use some of her great magic to get rid of the children for ever.

On a hot day she called the children to her and suggested a swim in Lough Derravaragh. Lir was busy with affairs of state so was delighted when Aoife told him where she and the children were going. He had begun to sense that all was not well with his new wife

and that she did not seem to enjoy
the company of his beloved children
as much as he did.

All was still by the lough side.

Even the birds were silent. But soon
the children were splashing and
laughing in the cool water. Aoife
walked slowly to the lapping
water's edge and raised her arms
and began to chant a powerful spell.
A cloud passed over the sun, a chill
wind whipped up white waves on

the lough and a crow shrieked
hoarsely. Finnuala turned to her
brothers in alarm but their faces
were masked in terror.

'Finnuala!' they shrieked.
'Finnuala, what is happening to
you?'

Even as they looked their beloved

sister turned into a swan before their eyes. Aoife continued her chanting and the wind grew stronger, rain began to fall and the boys too slowly turned into swans. There was a great flash of lightning – and all was calm again. The sun came out, the wind dropped and the birds began to sing. All was as before, except four pure white swans floated on the waters of the lough.

Aoife laughed triumphantly to herself.

'You will live as swans for nine hundred years, three hundred here on Lough Derravaragh, three hundred on the Sea of Moyle and three hundred on Inish Glora. You will not regain your human forms unless you hear the sound of a holy man's bell. Now I shall have Lir to myself,' and without a backwards glance she hurried away to find him.

But her magic was not as powerful as she thought. She had failed to still the human voices of the children. Finnuala called her brothers to her side and bid them be brave.

'Our father will not leave us here to pine and weep. He has all the powers of the Tuatha Dé Danann.

He will rescue us. Have courage,
my brothers!'

Aoife told Lir that his children had
drowned in the lough.

'Do not worry, my husband. I will look after you and we will be happier than we have ever been.'

But Lir pushed away her clinging arms and ran like the wind to the lough side, calling his children's names. Of his beloved children there was no sign but as he sank to his knees by the water's edge the four swans glided up. Lir was weeping and murmuring their names when he heard his Finnuala speaking to him.

'Dearest father, we are here. We have not drowned but Aoife has transformed us into swans.'

Lir's anger was terrible to see. He

ran into Aoife's chamber where she
sat calmly brushing her long black
hair.

'What is this great wickedness you
have done? You must release my
children from this evil spell at once,'
he raged.

But Aoife continued brushing her
long black hair.

'I cannot undo the spell, my
beloved husband,' she said sweetly,
'but what do the children matter?
You and I can be together now.'

Lir could now see what an evil

woman Aoife was. He seized her by the arm and called on all his ancient magic and the power of his ancestors and with a great clap of thunder she turned into a demon of the air. But Finnuala and her brothers were still trapped in the form of swans. Lir sat by the shores of the lough, speaking gently to his children and smoothing their white feathers. He tried all the spells he could think of, but he could not release them from Aoife's wickedness. Days and days he sat. The days turned into weeks and months and still Lir would not leave his children. He would sleep by

night and spend the days talking to
the swans. And so the years passed
and eventually Lir died, a sad and
lonely old man.

His swan children wept for him,

but Finnuala gathered her brothers
to her side and promised to keep
them safe come what may. Years and
years passed. People forgot about
Lir and his swan children but still
Finnuala watched over her brothers.
Three hundred years passed and the

swans left the lough to fly to the Sea of Moyle. It was bitterly cold and the poor swans were battered by icy winds and freezing hail. Finnuala sang to her brothers and reminded them of the happy days they had shared with their father before Aoife

came to tear them apart. This was a
desolate time for the little family but
somehow another three hundred
years passed and they flew south-
west to Inish Glora. They were tired
and old now and welcomed the
warmth of the summer sunshine but
their hearts were frozen with
sadness. They spoke little now, but
whenever they did, Finnuala
reminded her brothers of the last
words of Aoife's curse. One day
they would be released by the
sound of a holy man's bell.

At this time St Patrick had come to
Ireland and was travelling the
country preaching and building

small churches wherever he rested.
One of his followers came to Inish
Glora and built a tiny church there
and so it happened that one still
evening Finnuala and her brothers
heard a distant sound. It was the

clear high ringing of a bell.

'Come, my dearest brothers! Our torment is nearly at an end. We must go ashore and find the holy man.'

And find him they did. As he listened to their story he reached out

94

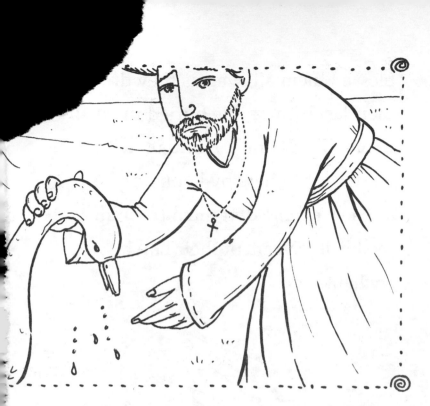

his hand to stroke their heads and
slowly the feathers drifted away and
Finnuala and her brothers stood
before him. They were old, so old,
white haired and wrinkled, no
longer young healthy children and
all were nigh to death. The holy man

blessed them all even as they dre
their last breaths. He buried them a..
in one grave, brave Finnuala with
her three brothers by her side, just
as she had shielded them through
the terrible years of their harsh
enchantment.